Lucy Lie-a-lot

Irene Howat

For Victoria and Gabriela

Christian Focus Publications

Lucy Lie-a-lot had a very kind teacher.

Her name was Miss Rosy.

The class had two pet goldfish called Round and About.

They were called Round and About because they swam round and about the fish bowl all day long.

It was autumn in Miss Rosy's class. 'Please, Miss,' said Tommy. 'We're going to have a new baby.'

Lucy's hand shot up. 'We're having a new baby too,' lied Lucy-Lie-a-lot.

As she skipped home from school Lucy's lie was like a balloon filled with sticky yellow custard. It kept getting in the way of her skipping.

It was winter and newstime in Miss Rosy's class.

'Please, Miss,' said Tommy. 'At the hospital I saw a scan photo of our baby.'

Lucy's hand shot up. 'So did I, and we're having twins,' lied Lucy Lie-a-lot.

As she hopped home from school that day, Lucy's red lie balloon seemed to fill up with more sticky yellow custard. It kept getting in the way of her hopping.

It was springtime in Miss Rosy's class. 'Please, Miss,' said Tommy. 'My mum cleaned up my old cot for the baby.'

'My mum bought a shiny new one,' lied Lucy Lie-a-lot.

As she cycled home from school that day Lucy's red lie balloon seemed to grow and grow. It was full of even more sticky yellow custard. It kept getting in the way of her wheels.

It was summer and newstime in Miss Rosy's class. 'Please, Miss,' said Tommy. 'I've got a new baby sister!'

Lucy's hand shot up. 'I've got twin brothers,' lied Lucy Lie-a-lot. The goldfish opened their mouths in surprise!

As she danced home from school that day Lucy's red lie balloon was so full of sticky yellow custard Lucy was sure that it would burst.

Lucy had to stop dancing because it kept getting in her way.

It was Sports Day in Miss Rosy's class.

'How are the twins?' Miss Rosy asked Lucy's mum.

Suddenly Lucy Lie-a-lot's balloon burst and covered her in sticky yellow custard that only she could see. The only bit of Lucy that wasn't yellow was her face.

It was very, very red.

God is truth and he wants us always to tell the truth and never to tell lies.

Dear Father in heaven,

please help me to tell the truth, and to say sorry if I do tell a lie. Please make me more like Jesus who never, ever told lies.

Amen.

'I have chosen the way of truth; I have set my heart on your laws.' Psalm 119:30

Jesus said 'I am the way and the truth and the life. No-one comes to the Father except through me.' John 14:6

Collect the Little Lots Series
and answer these questions

Lucy Lie-a-lot

Where are the goldfish
called Round and About?

Harry Help-a-lot

What does Cheery Boy
the canary like to do?

Bobby Boast-a-lot

Is Champion the bravest
dog around?

Granny Grump-a-lot

How many mice has
Hunter the cat caught?

Lorna Look-a-lot

What interesting thing
has Sniff the dog found?

William Work-a-lot

How did Stuff the
hamster get his name?

Published by Christian Focus Publications,
Geanies House, Fearn, Tain, Ross-shire, IV20 1TW, Scotland.
www.christianfocus.com © Copyright 2005 Irene Howat Illustrated by Michel de Boer * Printed in the U.K.
The Little Lots series looks at positive and negative characteristics and values.
These titles will help children understand what God wants from our everyday lives. Other titles in this series include:
Lorna Look-a-lot; Granny Grump-a-lot; William Work-a-lot; Harry Help-a-lot; Bobby Boast-a-lot